MR. *EX* PRESIDENT

Roger Mee-Senseless

Meet Donald. Donald was a normal 8 year old boy who liked normal 8 year old boy things like:

Chasing girls,
Eating junk food,
Fast cars,
Picking bogies and flicking them.

He also loved money. Oh yeh, there was one thing that was not normal about 8 year old Donald.

He was a millionaire.

BADOING

lots and lots and
lots and lots and
lots and lots *
of cash

* and lots

His dad, Fred, was a real estate developer in New York. In order to avoid paying taxes he gave Donald cheques for $200,000 a time.

You'd think that this would make Donald popular at school wouldn't you?

You'd be wrong...

He often tried to get children to play with him by flashing the cash around but he had limited success.

At playschool Donald's favourite thing to do was build walls out of lego. He once spent an entire day building a huge wall across the width of the classroom.

He declared it:

"The most impressive wall to have ever been built in this kindergarten. Everyone agrees they have never seen a wall like it."

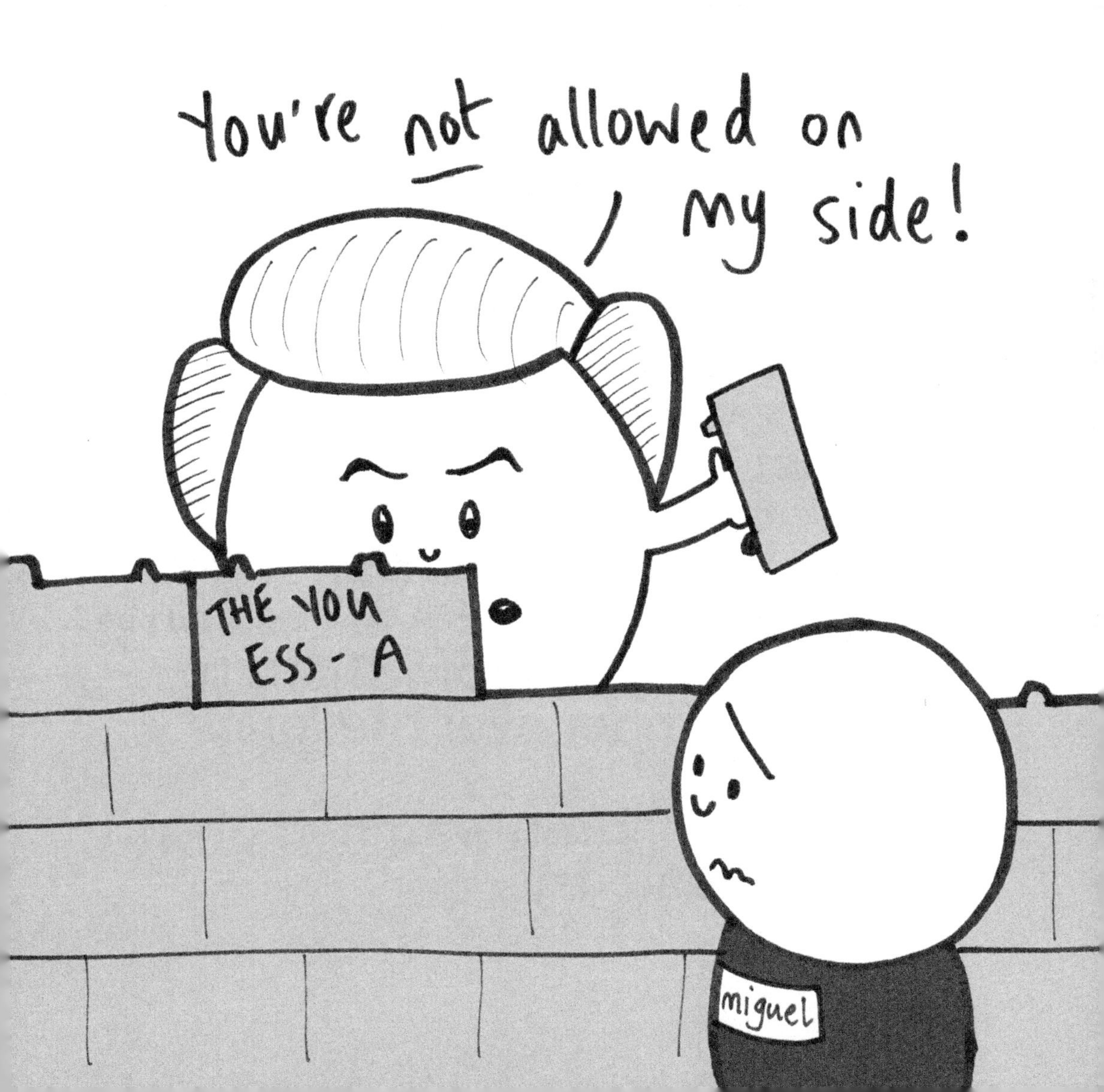
You're not allowed on my side!
THE YOU ESS - A
miguel

Donald alienated himself even more at dinner times. His absolute favourite food in the world was Cheetos. Closely followed by McDonalds, Burger King and Wendy's, washed down with an ice cold Diet Coke. Unfortunately these weren't on the menu at his kindergarten so he had arranged for one of his dad's drivers to come past every day at 12pm sharp to throw his dinner over the fence.

The other children watched on with a pang of jealousy.

When Donald was 8 he received his first written school report. He wasn't too pleased with it so he took his favourite wax crayon and wrote "FAKE NEWS" all over it.

"It's all fake, every single bit of it. It's all lies!" he told his parents when he got home. "I'm number one in my class, everyone agrees."

"No, we don't," said everyone else.

When Donald was 13 his father sent to a military boarding school.

This was to help teach him discipline. He learnt many skills there including; how to shine shoes, how to properly make a bed and how to bully people effectively.

He didn't know it at the time but these skills would come in useful later in his life (apart from the shoe shining and bed making).

MONDAY:

6 AM - ROLL CALL

8 AM - PARADE

10 AM - SELF PROMOTION

12 PM - MASTERCLASS -
HOW TO INSULT
LIKE A BAD ASS

When Donald was still a quite light shade of orange he had his first child who he named Donald, because one Donald Trump on this planet is evidently not enough.

He became a highly successful businessman after a small one million dollar loan from his father and only filed for bankruptcy an outstanding 6 times.

This led to him being asked to star in 'The Apprentice' TV series and also the 'Junior Apprentice'.

you're a disgrace to the human race - you're fired.
JUNIOR APPRENTICE

Years later, when Donald was a very old man he and decided he wanted to become, in his own words, "The most importantist man in the whole wide world." And so, he decided to enter the race to become the next president of the USA.

His first job was to start wearing a hat with 'Make America Great Again' on it. Donald was very proud of the slogan and said that he should copyright it, even though it had been used by Ronald Reagan 36 years before.

Unbelievably, Donald won the election. He graciously accepted the honour by running around the room in his y-fronts using his hand to make an 'L' on his forehead whilst shouting:

"LOOOOOOOOOSSSERS!"

Donald couldn't wait to put his lego expertise into practice and start building his much talked about wall.

On his first day as 'the most importantist man in the world', Donald awoke early so that he had time to make his hair look extra coiffered.

This involved a team of people tweeking and teasing with a range of special instruments. They began by rubbing an inflated balloon on a carpet and then passing it over his head to add volume. He had learnt this tip from the British Prime Minister, Boris Johnson.

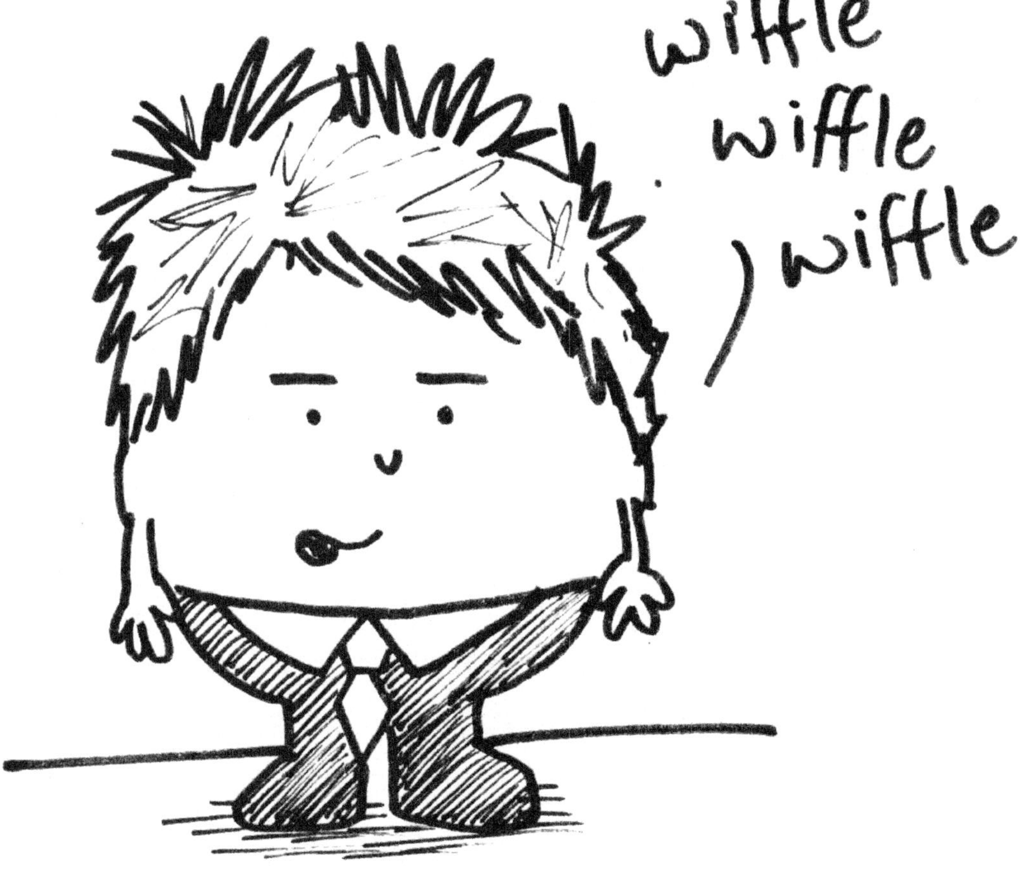

After a couple of hours his hair reached the required standard and the team could stand down. It was set in place using 4 and a half full cans of industrial hairspray.

The 1,642 cans of hair spray that he uses per year are thought to contribute to 3% of the world's entire greenhouse gas emissions. Donald's reliance on this product would lead to him pulling out of the Paris Climate Agreement.

Donald had lots of AMAZING ideas. One of his most amazingist was to renovate the White House, so it was more befitting for a man of his stature.

His plan was to build a 50 storey extension rising from the middle of the building. He would then rebrand it as 'Trump Towers 2'. The top floor would be a casino and the grounds would be relandscaped into a 9 hole pitch and putt golf course.

In 2020 Donald was confronted with a big problem. A worldwide pandemic has taken hold and was killing many people. At the time there was no known cure or vaccine but Donald had a great idea to solve the problem...

"Inject disinfectant into yourself. It'll kill the virus in one minute flat. Or use some kind of light inside the body, maybe a glowstick up the bum or something."

This led to some other great ideas...

If you're suffering from stubborn constipation then simply insert some 'Trump inc dynamite' up your butt and blast it out!

INSTRUCTIONS
① Insert into anus
② light fuse
③ adopt the brace position
Dyna mite teehee
!

On the other hand, If you've got a bout of diarrhea then don't worry. All you need is a carrot of an appropriate girth and stick that up the same way as the dynamite.

Some of Donald's ideas didn't involve putting something up your bum but I can't think of any right now.

INSERT THIS END FIRST

After having such superb ideas Donald needed to recharge his batteries so he decided to go for a round of golf.

Donald was a very good golfer, or so people thought. He employed a special caddy whose job it was to carry all of his clubs, drive the buggy, advise him on which shot to take and most importantly to scout ahead and move the ball into the centre of the fairway and 50 yards closer to the pin. He would then congratulate Donald on such an 'outstanding shot'.

SCORECARD — D. TRUMP

HOLE	PAR	SCORE
1	3	1
2	4	2
3	3	2
4	5	4
5	3	2
6	4	0
7	4	1
8	5	3
9	3	2

H	P	S
10	5	3
11	3	2
12	3	1
13	4	1
14	2	-1
15	5	2
16	4	3
17	3	2
18	4	3

TOTAL 33 (new world record)

Donald was bored so he decided to see what was on TV. After channel hopping for 30 minutes his wife asked him what he was looking for.
"Either: Ghosts can't do it, The Little Rascals, Zoolander or Home Alone 2."
"They're all films that you're in aren't they?" said his wife.
"PURE COINCIDENCE!" came Donald's reply.
Donald didn't watch the news because it was 'all fake anyway, apart from maybe FOX, who offer a very balanced view.'

Donald hadn't been for a spray tan for 2 days so he decided to go for a top up. He sat down in the reception area and leafed through the catalogue to select his colour choice.

His favourite was 'Jaffa' or 'Creosote'. He couldn't quite decide between the two but because he was such a special client the salon agreed to allow him to mix colours together for a unique shade. Donald said that this was 'the biggest honour of his life so far.' "Really? Bigger than the honour of being made president?" asked the assistant.

"Oh yeh, I forgot about that," said Donald.

"And do you know what?" continued Donald, "I think 50 Shades of Orange is the greatest book I've ever read. Apart from maybe the bible or 'The Art of the Deal' by me, although I haven't actually read that but I've heard it is outstanding. Yes - 50 Shades of Orange, definitely better than the Quran, maybe the publishers could use that as a quote on the cover."

in 2021 there was a US election. Donald's rules for this were pretty simple:

If I win then all is fine.

If I don't win then everything and everyone is corrupt and it is all FAKE and I will sue anyone who says otherwise.

Unfortunately for him, he didn't win.

Although he did go down in history as a record making president. The record in question was becoming
the first US president to be impeached, twice.

He was, however, aquitted. Something which Donald thought was tremendous.

Printed in Great Britain
by Amazon